# ONE LAST KISS

A STONEVIEW STORIES NOVELLA

LOLA KING

*Copyright © 2023 by Lola King*
*All rights reserved. No part of this publication may be reproduced, stored or transmitted in any form or by any means, electronic, mechanical, photocopying, recording, scanning, or otherwise without written permission from the publisher. It is illegal to copy this book, post it to a website, or distribute it by any other means without permission.*
*This novel is entirely a work of fiction. The names, characters and incidents portrayed in it are the work of the author's imagination. Any resemblance to actual persons, living or dead, events or localities is entirely coincidental. Designations used by companies to distinguish their products are often claimed as trademarks. All brand names and product names used in this book and on its cover are trade names, service marks, trademarks and registered trademarks of their respective owners. The publishers and the book are not associated with any product or vendor mentioned in this book. None of the companies referenced within the book have endorsed the book.*
*All songs, song titles an lyrics contained in this book are the property of the respective songwriters and copyright holders.*

*Cover art by Wild Love Designs*
*Alpha reading by Lauren Pixley*

# CONTENT WARNING

This book is not recommended to readers under the age of 18. This is a dark bully romance and contains scenes that some readers may find triggering. If this is something you are not comfortable with, please do not go any further.

For a full list of triggers, please contact Lola at lolaking.books@gmail.com

Enjoy!
Lots of love,

Lola ♡

# PLAYLIST

*Violets* - Josh Golden
*Would've, Could've, Should've* - Taylor Swift
*Overwhelmed* - Royal & the Serpent
*Battle Scars* - MOD SUN
*Lie to me* - Tate McRae, Ali Gatie
*Love Runs Out* - Martin Garrix, G-Eazy, Sasha Alex Sloan
*Electric Love* - BØRNS

# 1

JAMIE

*Violets - Josh Golden*

Steam pours out of our small bathroom as Jake opens the door. I'm in our kitchen, putting two plates of garlic fried rice, eggs, and hot dogs on the table. Who knew Filipino breakfast would become one of Jake's favorites?

Walking out of the bathroom with nothing but a towel around his waist, he inhales deeply. "Mm...smells good in here."

"Don't get used to it," I tell him as I cross the small room to meet him. "I just had to keep myself busy so I wouldn't freak out."

"Freak out about what?" He grabs my waist and pulls me up, dropping a wet kiss on my lips. His hair drips onto my green dress and I try to push him away, but he tightens his grip.

"Jake! I just got dressed, don't get me wet!" I moan a complaint.

"But I love having you all wet," he smiles against my lips.

He straightens up and lets me go. "What's wrong, baby? Why are you freaking out?"

I point at the kitchen table. Two sealed envelopes rest between our plates.

Our gazes cross and the world stops for a minute. Drowning in his midnight eyes, I forget about the anxiety I've been wrapped in all morning.

"Alright," he nods, understanding what's going on. "I'm going to get dressed and we're going to open these together."

I nod silently and wrap my hands around both his biceps before squeezing, loving the hardness.

He makes a little show out of flexing them to make me laugh before heading for the bedroom.

"I can't believe Maganda," he huffs as he closes the door to the bedroom. "I got you a dog so she would protect you, and she spends most of her days hiding in our bed."

"Leave my girl alone," I scold him as he approaches the table.

"Alright," he says once we're both sitting. My leg is bouncing under the table and he puts a firm hand on it. "What do we have here?" He looks down at the envelopes. "Grossman and Silver Falls." He scratches the heavy stubble he now sports all the time.

"I don't like this," I murmur. "I don't like this at all."

I applied to eight med schools. And I already got rejected by five of them. Some of them weren't even my favorites to begin with—their location really wasn't ideal—but they were amazing schools, and I was heartbroken when they denied me. I've always been the best student in my year. I was Stoneview Prep's Valedictorian. But college has been a completely different experience. I was freshly in love and happy in freshman year and I didn't focus as much as I should have. It wasn't only that, the level at our college is much higher than I ever expected. I work all the time, I do study groups, and I miss out on sleep because I stay at the library until midnight most nights. My Biochem professor has become my best friend and I spend most of his office hours with him. He's helped me so much to try and keep my GPA high. It's not been enough, though. Because after going to two rounds of interviews, I was still denied by Harvard, George Washington, Brown, Stanford, and Florida state.

I know they're the absolute best med schools, but that's what I've always wanted and expected for myself.

Now we're staring at NYU Grossman School of Medicine and Silver Falls University. Both would be amazing for the location, the reputation, the fact that I would graduate from two of the very best.

But if I don't get in? I have no contingency plan because I'm a total idiot who thought she was smart enough for the top schools in the country and didn't even apply to average schools.

"Oh my gosh, how could I be so stupid?" I whimper, my head falling into my hands.

"Angel," Jake says as he captures my hands and pulls them away from my face. "Let's take a deep breath."

Instead of listening, I escape his hold, snap the Grossman envelope and rip it open.

"Okay, or you could just ignore me. Let's do this."

My hands are shaking as I pull out the letter and my eyes scan it. "Dear Ms. Williams," I read in a mumble, "It is with sincere regret...*no*," I cry out.

I snap into a standing position so fast the kitchen chair falls behind me. "Why?!" I shriek. "The interview went so well..." I rip the letter into shreds and throw it in the bin.

"Angel," Jake says softly as he gets up and joins me. He wraps his arms around me from the back. His heat and huge presence behind me makes me feel so protected it helps hold back the tears. "This isn't the last one. There's still a chance. In fact, there are still two chances."

"I can't believe this. I'm never going to become a doctor."

"Hey, I don't want to hear any of this." He turns me around, grabs my waist and sits me on the kitchen counter. "You are the smartest, most gorgeous, hardworking woman I've ever had the chance to meet. Everything will be fine. I know it, Jamie."

"You don't know anything." I bring the tip of my fingers to my eyes, dabbing away tears before they fall off my eyelids. He pulls my hands away and holds my face between his, his thumbs pressing against my tear ducts.

"I know *everything*," he insists with a small smile. "I know the energy you put into your passion. I know the late nights spent working. The extra reading, the research. I *know*, Angel, that those schools were mistaken to reject you."

He runs his nose against mine and I sniffle. "Everyone already knows where they're going next year. Sophie got accepted into Harvard! Josh is going to UCLA. Chris already knows he'll be in Yale's law school. Everyone's going on to do great things and I'm the only one left."

"Angel," he says sternly as he grabs my jaw, forcing me to look at him. "You're spiraling. We don't want that. Just take a deep breath for me."

My hand wraps around his wrist, but he doesn't move, his fingers digging into my skin.

"I—"

"I *said* take a deep breath. Now."

Trembling, I open my mouth slightly and take a deep breath before letting it out.

"Good girl. Close your mouth. Inhale through your nose for four seconds."

I do so, not thinking about anything else but the calm sound of his orders. "Block for seven." I hold my breath as I count in my head. "Exhale through your mouth for eight."

I do and look up at him. "I don't feel better." Even though the trembling and sobbing is gone, I can feel my mind trying to fight me. I can't stop thinking about that letter on the table behind Jake.

"You know we have ways to make you forget about the stress," he murmurs before his lips come to kiss my neck.

My head falls to the side to give him more access. "So either you calm down," he says between kisses. "Or I can make you."

His strong hands wrap around my thighs. So high that I feel the pressure between my legs.

"Jake," I whisper just before his lips crash against mine. His tongue demands entry and I open gladly. Subconsciously, my body comes closer to his and my crotch slams into him, sending a zap of electricity through me.

"Okay," I nod as he takes a break from kissing me. "Make me. Make me calm down."

He chuckles against my lips. "I don't believe that's how we do things, Angel."

My heart drops to my stomach as another shiver courses through me. "Make me...please."

"Mm," he smiles. "That's much better. Stand by the table."

He takes a step back and I'm on my feet. I take the short steps that separate me from the table and lift up my dress. I'm about to bend over, ready for him to fuck me from behind but he grabs me by the hair and pulls me back. "Did I say bend over like a whore or did I say stand by the table?"

My breath disappears, stuck in my chest and mixing with the tension there. "The...I..."

"You're not going to get fucked, Angel. You're going to forget about your very mere existence. Get on your knees and crawl under the table."

*Oh gosh.*

We've done this before, the week I took my exams. I don't know how long I spent cock-warming him. Long enough to forget about anything going on in my life.

He sits down where I had set up our breakfast and watches me as I get under the table.

"Take my cock out, Angel," he orders with a casual tone as I see him reach for his phone in his pocket. He spreads his legs and I settle between them on my knees. I undo his belt and unzip his jeans, my thighs tense with anticipation. He's semi-hard already.

I wrap my lips around him and his hand comes to grab my hair. "No. Sucking," he says low. "Here's your challenge; don't get me hard. Do, and our game is over."

As if this is fair. Jake sometimes gets hard by the mere sight of me walking around fully clothed. It's imagining the wicked things he'll do to me that gets him hard.

I wrap my lips around his base and make sure not to lick him, and to keep my teeth away. I'm forced to relax my jaw as my nose presses against his crotch.

I breathe him in, relishing in everything that makes him the man he is.

I shift on my knees as soon as I feel drool coming out of my mouth.

"Stay still down there," I hear from above the table. "Got a phone call to make."

A second later, he's on the phone with Chris, asking him if he boarded his plane already. We're all celebrating my birthday tonight in Stoneview. Except I haven't exactly been in the mood for it. Jake's hand in my hair tightens, silently ordering me to concentrate on my task.

I close my eyes and focus on his warmth, his smell, and the way my body aches for him to touch me.

I like our games. Over time, they've become sexier and dirtier. He keeps me on my toes and knows what I love. Nobody can satiate my being with twisted pleasure the way Jake White does.

I can feel myself getting wetter the longer I keep him in my mouth without being able to do anything. This isn't teasing just for him, the anticipation for me is unbearable because I know that if he's satisfied, he'll make sure I not only forget about my current stress but the entire world.

I'm not sure how long it's been when I feel him shift. My eyes are heavy, my jaw aching. All I know is that he suddenly pushes against me and I feel his dick growing harder in my mouth.

I try to pull away, not wanting him to make me lose our game, but his hand comes to the back of my head.

When his other hand comes to brush my nipple above my dress, I moan around him and feel him hiss above the table. He thrusts into my mouth and pulls out suddenly, his hard cock bobbing as it springs free.

"Aw, Angel," he mocks as he pulls his chair away and looks down at me. "It's game over for you, baby."

He grabs the collar of my dress and drags me up until I'm in front of the table. I feel hazy, and when I notice that he ate his entire food I look back at him, my eyes unfocused. When did he eat? How long has it been?

He grabs my hips, turns me around and pushes against

my back until I slam against the table, making everything rattle.

He pushes my dress up and the first slap against my ass cheeks makes me shriek. "Didn't I say not to get me hard?"

"You th—"

"Don't put yourself in more trouble," he growls. He knows he's being unfair, but he also knows I love it. He slaps my ass cheeks again and this time I only gasp. "Angel, I'm going to bury myself so deep inside you you're not gonna remember your own name."

With his foot, he kicks my legs apart before grabbing both my wrists in one hand and pushing them against the small of my back.

"Bite your lip, baby. We don't want another complaint from the neighbors."

He doesn't give me time, though. He drives inside me in a violent thrust that pushes my hips against the table. Our cheap wooden table creaks as he accelerates, but it doesn't resonate nearly as loudly as my moans.

"Jake..." I whimper. "Slow down."

Sometimes, he forgets that no matter how wet he makes me, his size isn't exactly the easiest to take.

He pulls away slightly and rolls his hips, hitting less deep and slower. "Oh..." I gasp as he hits my g-spot. I push on my toes, meeting his strokes. "Jake..." This time my moan is languid as I feel a fire igniting my whole body.

"Angel, listen to me," he says as he slows down. I whine a complaint and he slaps my ass again. "I want you to stop thinking so low of yourself every time you get some bad news."

"Stop talking about this," I grunt as I push against him.

He thrusts into me harshly and my knees buckle as I

scream. He catches me at the waist and keeps me tight against him.

"Tell me you're smart."

"Jake, please, stop..." My cheeks flush and embarrassment makes me feel unstable. I hate when he makes me do this.

"Say, I am a smart and beautiful woman."

He rolls his hips and I moan. "I don't...just stop with this."

I feel him stiffen behind me. He pulls out of me and his annoyance burns through me. "Wait—"

I'm too late. He grabs me by the hair and presses my face against the table. "Don't fucking tell me to stop when I'm telling you how fucking incredible you are, Jamie. It annoys me." He slams into me, making me scream out in pleasure and pain.

His other hand comes around me and he pinches my clit harshly. "Ah!! Jake..." I cry out.

"I can't fucking hear you. Say, I am a smart and beautiful woman."

"I...I..." I whimper from overwhelming pleasure when he starts stroking my clit. It's hypersensitive and pulsing from when he pinched me. Each stroke from his fingers is driving me mad. "I'm a smart...anngh...Jake..."

"Try again," he murmurs just above me.

"I'm a smart and beautiful...woman!" I scream as I explode from his fingers and his dick working simultaneously on my pleasure.

Despite my shattering orgasm, he takes his time as he keeps driving into me. He rolls his hips, making me moan loudly. He keeps the flame of sensuality burning through my veins and spends time pleasuring himself using my body.

"You are perfect, Angel," he growls as he starts accelerating. "You're everything I could ever ask for and more. I don't care what a fucking board of admission thinks. You're a queen and I won't ever let you think any less of yourself." His sentence dies on a hiss as he comes inside me in a brutal assault.

A plate smashes on the floor and startles me. My legs give up under my weight and Jake catches me, before walking us to the bathroom.

He helps me undress and does the same before we both get in the shower. He washes me slowly and I watch him with a dumb grin.

"What?" he chuckles as he catches my loving stare.

"I don't deserve you," I murmur. "You're too good to me."

"Why? Because I think you're the most amazing woman that's ever walked this earth?"

"Stop," I giggle. I slap his chest and shake my head. "It's just...I could have spent the whole day sulking, but you didn't let me. You...*believe* in me. I love you for it."

"Angel," he smiles down at me as he puts the loofah to the side. "You believed in me at a moment of my life I had completely given up on myself. The least I can do is show you a fraction of what that feels like."

"I love you," I say before slamming my lips against him.

"I love you too."

I get out of the shower before him and wrap a towel around myself. I pick up my dress from the bathroom floor and bring my phone from the kitchen to the bedroom with me. I tap the screen as I'm putting underwear on and my heart stops.

There's a text from my Biochem professor.

## Chapter 1

> Professor Olson: Good morning, Jamie. I have a letter from admission office for you in my office. Letters will be sent in the new year, but since you told me you were in town between Christmas and New Year, please feel free to come by my office to pick it up.

"Oh my gosh," I gasp. "Jake!" Hope rises in my chest. If Professor Olson has my letter, it *must* be good news. I don't want to set myself up for disappointment, but I feel something different. This is the one. I studied for four years at this college. Olson has seen me give it my all and I know he has an influence on the med school admission board.

I put my dress back on, not even bothering with a bra and run to the living room. I grab my coat and handbag and scream toward the bathroom.

"I'm leaving! I love you!!"

# 2

## JAMIE

*Would've, Could've, Should've - Taylor Swift*

Running down our road, I hop on the first bus toward campus. I should have waited for Jake to get out of the shower and ask him to drive me, but I simply couldn't wait. I spend twenty minutes on the bus, my legs bouncing and biting my inner cheek. My hair is still wet from my shower, and I forgot to put a sweater on. 31$^{st}$ of December means freezing temperatures but I can't even feel the cold. I'm sweating from the stress and counting down the minutes until I can open my letter.

My phone rings and I watch Jake's cute pout appear on the screen. He only makes this face for me, and I feel lucky that I caught it in the picture.

"*Where are you?*" he snaps as soon as I pick up.

"I'm sorry. I said I was leaving but you probably didn't hear me in the shower."

Jake is living with the sort of trauma that makes him jump to the worst conclusion if I leave without letting him know. We've been through so much together it's been hard to accept and convince ourselves that the craziness was over and fate wasn't against us anymore. Nothing is a threat to us anymore, but you can't simply force your body and mind to stop being in survival mode. It takes time and he's worked hard at it, but leaving the apartment without letting him know wasn't exactly the best idea.

"Professor Olson said he had my letter from med school. I'm just on my way to meet him."

"*That guy uses any fucking excuse to bring you to his office,*" he complains.

"Stop being ridiculous."

"*If this meeting lasts any longer than the ten seconds it takes you to rip open an envelope and read the letter, I'll be showing up to his office too. Let's see how he likes that.*"

"Jake, please. This is important to me."

I hear him huff on the other side. "*We have a four-and-a-half-hour drive to Stoneview. Don't be long.*"

"Promise," I smile into the phone. "I love you."

"*I love you,*" he says sourly before hanging up.


As soon as I reach my professor's office, I knock on his door. He shouldn't be here and neither should I. We're on Christmas break and no one is in the building. He should be on vacation with his wife but he's a workaholic and today I love him for it. I knock on his office door with a trembling hand.

"Come in," he calls from behind.

"Hi," I smile brightly as I open the door. I stupidly feel like if I'm extra nice, maybe the words on the letter will change from 'We regret' to 'Congratulations'.

"Jamie, hi!" Professor Olson stands up from behind his desk and comes to me, shaking my hand. "How are you? I wasn't sure if you were going to come."

"I'm sorry, I should have answered your text. I was so excited I came right away."

He nods and smiles, before taking off his glasses.

Olson isn't the kind of professor I thought I would have in Biochem. He's young and handsome, nerdy in the finest way possible. A lot of girls in my class fall head over heels for him. He's around thirty-eight, married, and he told me not long ago that he and his wife were expecting. I always feel comfortable around him and I love spending time together sharing his knowledge.

"Well, don't get too excited because we don't actually know what that letter says."

"I know." I nod stiffly. "It's just…I've worked so hard and I keep getting rejected."

"The competition this year has been particularly tough," he tells me as he grabs the letter on his mahogany desk. "Only two of my five best students got a positive answer from top schools. I know yours is coming, Jamie. Don't worry."

"Is that Sophie and Josh?" I ask as I walk to him. My two good university friends got their acceptances and I didn't yet. I've been having conflicting feelings being happy for them while utterly envious at the same time.

"That's right. Come, let's open it," he says as he sits down on one of the two chairs opposite his desk.

My stomach twists from the confusion. Did I understand right?

"Open it, here? Now?"

"Of course," he chuckles.

## Chapter 2

"Oh," I shift uncomfortably on my feet as I put a hand on the back of the chair next to his. "I-I thought I'd just bring this home. I've opened all the other letters with my boyfriend. We made a sort of ritual out of it." A certain embarrassment comes over me. What am I doing? Talking about opening my letters with my boyfriend like a teenage girl waiting to see if she's going to go to the same college as him.

*You're twenty-two in less than twenty-four hours, Jamie. Act like it.*

"Your boyfriend?" he chuckles.

I run a hand behind my neck and bite my inner cheek. "I mean...It's silly, of course."

This makes nothing better. I now feel wrong for basically saying that Jake supporting me and being there for me to share the experience of opening my med school letters is *silly*.

"Well," he says as he tilts his head. "I should be with my pregnant wife right now, helping her prepare our New Year's Eve dinner, but I came here today because I knew your letter must have arrived. I care about you, Jamie. Truly. I'm your biggest supporter, probably more than your boyfriend." A small laugh comes out of him. "I'm joking, of course. But I would love to be with you when you open this."

That whole speech sounds so off it makes me want to take several steps back. But he's holding my precious med school letter in his hand, and I would feel so rude to leave without even taking it. I'm probably making it up. He's a decent man and I just haven't met many of those in my life. I tend to twist everything to bad intentions because of experience.

I sit down next to him and smile politely as I put my bag

on the floor. Understanding I'm agreeing with him he says, "I'm sure he'll understand."

I ignore the strange, icky feeling I'm getting and extend my hand to grab the letter from him. "May I?"

"Of course. Here." Our fingers touch and I shift in my seat, feeling uncomfortable. "Read it to me."

I open the letter with trembling hands, the feeling completely different than when I do it with Jake. I'm nervous, but mainly because Olson is watching me intently and I don't like it at all.

"Um," I hesitate. "Dear Miss Williams, due to an unprecedented increase in submitted applications, we updated your application status to...*waitlisted*?!" I choke. Disappointment washes over me and my arms drop to my lap. My fingers tighten around the piece of paper, creasing it and practically tearing it. "I don't understand," I push past my tight throat.

Now I'm uncomfortable, sad, and incredibly embarrassed that Olson has to witness all of it. I wish I hadn't done this. I wish I was at home with Jake so he could hold me again.

"Jamie," my professor sighs. "This isn't the worst outcome. At least there's hope."

I shake my head, forcing the tears to stay at bay and trying to act professional. "Of course," I rasp. "I...I'm just worried about my future."

"This isn't the end of the world," he reassures me. "I have a very good relationship with the admission committee and you're one of my top students. I can always make sure you get in."

My brows furrow as my eyes stay stuck to the letter on my lap. I can't make myself look at him as I lose my professionalism. "If you're so close to them, and you think I'm a top student, why didn't you say anything to them before? Why don't I have an acceptance letter?"

He chuckles to himself and I feel him move his chair closer. Leaning toward me he says, "Because that's not how life works, Jamie. Favors don't come for free. If you want my help, we can sort something out."

There's a brief pause as his hand comes to rest on my thigh and my entire body freezes.

"But that's for you to decide," he concludes.

"I..." My eyes are stuck on his hand. My dress is short, and I didn't even put tights on despite the cold. The rush made me leave the house half dressed. His hand is high enough that the tip of his fingers comes under the skirt of my dress.

My heart is beating fast and I can hear it drumming in my ears, rendering me practically deaf. Cold sweat starts running down my neck and I shake my head slightly.

"I..." I try again, but my throat is too dry to talk. "Professor Olson," I gulp.

"Don't look so scared." I can hear the smile in his voice, but I don't have the strength to look at him, my eyes glued to his hand. "You're a very pretty girl, Jamie. So tiny and breakable. It's adorable." His hand tightens and I let out a choked whimper. "I can do a lot of things for you. You just have to ask very nicely."

When I keep quiet for several seconds, he insists. "You understand what I'm saying, right? How badly do you want to go to med school, pretty girl?"

His grip tightens again, painfully so. I can feel the tip of his fingers bruising my skin, his nails pushing in.

In a moment of reality, I gasp and push myself off the chair. I fall to the side of it, attempting to escape his hold. Quickly I stand back up, grab my bag, and arrange my dress.

"I...have to go."

I stumble out of the room, running away, hurrying down the stairs and the long hallways of our building. The second I'm outside, I sprint.

I burst through our front door, frantically looking for Jake. As soon as I see him on the sofa, I explode into tears. Jake jumps over the back, his worried voice barely reaching past my sobs.

"Angel, what's wrong?"

I take a deep breath, ready to tell him everything, but I freeze.

It's Jake.

He will lose it. He will find Olson and destroy him in any way possible. Anyone who looks at me too closely gets a death look strong enough to make them run away. He won't rest until he feels he had the revenge he wanted on my professor, and he'll put himself in trouble for me. Undeniably.

The kind of anxiety I used to feel when I was in high school comes back to me. The horrible type where I feel stuck, and I have no way out. I can't bring this back to Jake. Our awful days are meant to be over.

I look at my boyfriend, his deep blue eyes search for something in mine and I shake my head.

Maybe I made it up. He didn't say anything clearly. Maybe I assumed he meant sexual favors.

I want to slap myself. I'm always reading articles about women who doubted themselves when they were clearly victims of abuse of power.

So why can't I see it clearly right now? Am I that naïve that I only think it happens to other people?

And his hand...

Maybe I was in such a state of shock over the waitlisting that everything was heightened. I thought his hand was high on my thigh but maybe he just put it on my knee and I saw it as an attack when it was nothing else but a reassuring gesture.

I don't even remember what he said exactly. Everything about that moment is blurry and I couldn't tell Jake for sure what happened.

Jake's strong arms wrap around me and he lifts me up, holding me close to him as he walks me to the sofa.

"Jamie," he says softly as he sits me down. He comes next to me and brushes wet strands of hair away from my face. "Talk to me."

I shake my head again and give him a small smile. "I'm so dramatic," I chuckle sadly, wiping tears away from my face. Realizing I'm still holding the crushed letter in my hand, I show it to him.

He reads it quickly and takes me tightly in his arms. "Baby," he whispers in my ear. "This is amazing news."

"No," I choke.

"We have to take this one step at a time, okay? This is an improvement."

"I'm sorry," I cry out. "I'm so sorry."

"What? What are you sorry about?"

"I should have never opened it without you." My arms wrap around his waist, and I bury myself into him.

He grabs my hips and pulls me until I'm straddling him. "It's okay," he says softly. "I'm not mad." He wipes my tears for the second time today and smiles at me. "No more talks about med school now, okay? We're gonna get ready for your birthday and to celebrate a new year. Then, we're going to drive to Stoneview, party with our friends, and forget about anything that upset you. Just for tonight. How does that sound?"

I nod and give him a small smile. "Sounds good."

"Alright." He runs his hands up and down my thighs, grabbing my panties. "Let's get ready before I rip these off."

# 3

## JAMIE

*Overwhelmed - Royal & the Serpent*

I'm not really focused when Jake parks his car in front of the Murrays' mansion. My gaze is lost ahead of me but all I can see is images of Olson, trying to recall if his gesture was inappropriate or not. I'm confused and lost, and I startle when Jake's hand comes to rest on my knee, shaking my leg.

"Earth to Jamie," he says lightly.

"Huh?"

"I was just saying Ozy's already here. I'm excited, let's go."

I look around us and recognize the white Range Rover that belongs to Sam, already parked in the round driveway.

He rounds the car and opens my door, helping me out by grabbing my hand. I wobble slightly on the high heels I decided to wear for the night.

"Did I tell you you look edible in that dress?" he murmurs as he kisses my cheek.

"I sort of got the gist when you bent me over the sofa before we left," I giggle. I'm wearing a silky short white dress that contrasts beautifully with my skin. I put a hand on his chest and go on my toes to drop a kiss on his lips.

I'm a horrible person.

How could I go to Olson's office and open my letter with him when I know Jake and I have been opening all the other ones together. How could I let him put his hand on my thigh? I didn't move. I didn't say anything. I just...froze. That makes me feel just as guilty as him.

*He wasn't being inappropriate*, I repeat in my head. *You misunderstood. There's nothing to worry about.*

When I come out of my mental fight, Jake has already dragged me to the door. He grabs his keys and opens it, pulling me inside with him. I lose focus when my phone beeps in my handbag. I take it out and my breath cuts short when I see I've got a text from Olson.

> Professor Olson: You didn't seem against me helping you, Jamie. I can move you up the wait list.

I shake my head, trying to understand how he could have possibly come to the conclusion that I wasn't against him helping.

*Because you froze! You didn't say no!*
I didn't say anything.

> Professor Olson: No one has to know.

I struggle to take another breath, but I don't get a chance to think further about it because a form jumps on me.

"'Me!!" Emily shrieks as she wraps me in her arms and holds me so tightly she practically breaks my ribs.

My arms come around her and I relax into her hold.

"Oh gosh, I missed you," I breathe out into her ear.

## Chapter 3

When we finally separate, we look into each other's teary eyes as we hold hands.

"I need to know everything about that Juilliard asshole who tried to break your heart," I say seriously. "And about your graduation show. You know I'll be there. Your invite is on my fridge."

Like me, Emily is about to finish her senior year of college. She's already partly living her dream, having been dancing at Juilliard for four years.

"Oh, I have so much to talk about when it comes to this asshole. But I also need to tell you about my bitchy alternate who tried to push me off stage."

My mouth drops open. "It's a long story," she laughs as she waves her hand. "What about med schools? Any other replies?"

"Hi to you too, Em," Jake jumps in. "Can we get inside the house before we start spilling all that tea?"

Em's laugh doubles and she gives Jake a quick hug. "I am so stealing your girlfriend tonight."

"We'll see about that," he smiles as he puts a possessive hand behind my neck.

But as soon as we walk into the living room, my perfect boyfriend drops me for the only girl he loves as much as me.

"Ozy!" he exclaims as he goes to her and grabs her in a chokehold.

"Argh, fuck off!" I hear her fighting back. He messes with her hair before grabbing her into a tight hug.

"I missed you too," he smiles.

My heart melts when she hugs him back.

I say hi to Rose and her partners, Lik, Sam, and Rachel. Lik is as chatty as usual, Rachel stuck to Rose's side, and Sam the same silent man who looks like he's only here because Rose is.

Luke is next to join us. He came with his sister, Ella, and...

"Holy shit, she's hotter in real life," Emily mumbles in my ear before I can even process the gorgeous model he brought with him.

I'm not sure how Emily feels when she sees him with other girls. Luke is the same man he's always been, changing girlfriends every three to nine weeks as if they always come with a 'best before' date. I don't agree with his behavior, but he's on the other side of the country and we don't really get to talk about it.

All I see is paparazzi pictures of him online, always snapping the 'most eligible billionaire' with the latest top model, movie star, or empire heiress.

"Wait, do you know who she is?" I ask Em.

"Duh, 'Me. That's Elena Poraski. She's the new face of Chanel."

"Oh...I didn't know that," I whisper. "Wow."

"No, of course you didn't because they don't put Chanel in medicine books. We've got different interests," she chuckles.

"Em," Luke smiles, cutting off our exchange. "'Me." He gives each of us a hug before turning to his top model girlfriend. "This is Elena, my girlfriend. Elena, this is Emily and Jamie. Jamie's Jake's girlfriend. We all went to high school together."

"Hi," she smiles warmly at both of us. "It's so nice that you guys have all stayed friends since school."

"Where did you go to high school?" I ask politely.

"Oh, I was back home in Poland, then." Which would explain the accent.

"I bet the weather is different than L.A." Em adds.

"Oh, you girls met Elena," Rose says as she wraps an arm

around my waist. "Her and Luke have been in love for like a whole week," she smiles mockingly.

I pinch my lips to try and not laugh in front of Luke's girlfriend.

"Rose," Luke snarls. "I will tackle you to the floor. I hope you know that."

Sam is on the other side of the room, listening to Rachel, Lik, and Jake talking, but his gaze is on us in a split second like he heard Luke's threat very clearly.

"Yeah," Emily snorts. "I wouldn't advise that in front of the beast over there."

"She's the one this time, man," Rose insists as she slaps Luke's shoulder.

Luke's younger sister, Ella, says hi to everyone and comes to join her brother.

"Where's Chris?" she asks.

"Arguing with his lovely girlfriend in a different room so we don't have to be subjected to the awkwardness of their relationship," Rose answers deadpan.

"Ouch," Emily laughs.

As if he could hear us talking about him, Chris walks back into the room hand in hand with Megan. Aka, the harpy.

Absolutely everyone detests her. And it all came from her own behavior toward all of us. She's found something to criticize about everyone in this room and her bitchy personality is just another reminder of the Stoneview girls we left behind. She contrasts so sharply with Chris we're still all wondering what he is doing with her.

Chris pauses as soon as he enters. His eyes go to Ella, taking her in, and his mouth opens slightly. Megan tugs at his hand but he's completely forgotten about her.

Jake told me what had happened behind Luke's back.

That Chris and Ella dated secretly when we were in senior year and she was a freshman.

A lot of time has passed since. I thought he had moved on. Looking at him now, it seems I was wrong. He strides toward us, as if he can't stop himself and only manages to stop just before grabbing Luke's sister.

"Ella," he murmurs as if she was a divine apparition. He runs a hand through his hair, messing it up and then behind his neck, seemingly collecting himself. "Hi," he smiles politely. "I...didn't know you were coming. What a lovely surprise."

He pulls her into a hug, and we all notice Megan's dark look, which makes everyone feel uncomfortable.

Chris says hi to everyone else and we're all subjected to Megan's stare when he gives us a hug. "Guys, let's have dinner," he smiles at everyone.

Rose's eyes narrow on Megan and Luke has to elbow her in the ribs. "Stop it," he says in a low voice.

"Notice how he's perfected the unhappy smile since he failed to break up with her for the fourth time," she replies as Megan walks away.

"Four?" Emily chokes. "Does she give him a love potion or something?"

"I bet she's gonna manage to marry him or some shit like that," Rose adds.

"Talking about marriage," I smile brightly, trying to take the topic of conversation away from the harpy. I grab Rose's left hand and point at the beautiful engagement ring Rachel got her two years ago. "When's the big day? I haven't received an invite yet."

"I still can't believe *Rose White* has an engagement ring around her finger," Emily sighs. "Who knew God allowed such things."

"Took three of them to lock her down," Luke snorts.

"Em," Rose smiles brightly. "Don't be so sad. I can always check with Rach, Lik, and Sam if they'd be open to a fifth person joining us."

"Stop it," Em laughs, but her cheeks tint a deep red. She's always had a crush on Jake's twin.

Rose turns back to me. "No date yet. Nothing before I graduate."

The word *graduate* twists my stomach and I turn around to grab a flute of champagne on the nearby table. I need to forget about not only my future, but the present problem with Professor Olson.

We're eating our starters, all sitting around the long dining table, when something comes to my mind. "Where's Juliette?" I ask Chris. His younger adopted sister rarely travels with their parents.

Rose dramatically slaps a hand against her heart and looks at me. "Don't even mention it," she says. "She's at a *sleepover* for New Year's Eve." She's sitting between Lik and Sam while Rachel is opposite her, to my left.

Because Jake and Rose were Chris's foster siblings, Juliette ended up with two older brothers and one older sister. The protection they cast over her would scare the bravest warriors.

"They grow up too fast," Jake adds in a mock sob, to my right. "Can you imagine she's eleven already? What if she tries to kiss someone soon? Thank fuck there are no boys at that sleepover. We would have had to scare them all away."

Rachel and Rose let out a small laugh in unison. "Sure," Rachel nods. "No boys at sleepovers definitely stopped me from kissing," she teases him.

Jake's eyes widen, realizing how naïve his words were. "Oh my god...I'm gonna have to scare all the girls away too. Chris." He turns to his best friend. "Make a list of all her closest friends."

We all burst into laughter as Chris lifts a hand.

"We are not making a list of her closest friends. She'll be fine. It's only down the road," Chris reassures him. "If she needs anything we're a five-minute drive away."

My phone beeps next to my plate and as soon as I see Olson's name, my hand darts to turn it around so the screen is facing down. My eyes go to Jake, checking if he noticed anything, but he's now making conversation with Luke and Elena.

My shoulders sag as a breath escapes me. My gaze crosses with Sam's, sitting right in front of me. His eyes go to my phone then back at me, raising an eyebrow.

I gulp, not knowing what to do. The guy has always frightened me, and him being happily in love with Rose doesn't change much to the way he makes me feel.

"I need to use the bathroom," I murmur to whoever is near enough to hear me as I get up and grab my phone.

I escape to the hallway and hurry to the nearest bathroom. As soon as I'm locked in there, I look at the text from Olson.

> Professor Olson: Jamie, please don't ignore me. I would hate to be forced to tell the rest of the faculty that you came on to me.

A gasp escapes me before I slam my hand against my mouth to calm myself down. This can't be happening. Everything was fine in my life. Graduation and med school felt like a normal problem to have. This...this feels too much like I'm cursed.

## Chapter 3

I type a reply with trembling hands. I erase and retype random words multiple times, trying to think of anything that would calm him down.

In the end, I decide to bide my time.

> Jamie: Please, I'm not ignoring you. I'm busy with family tonight. Can we talk about this when I come back from the break, please?

I send and read it again. I hate myself for the number of *please's* in there. Why am I begging him when he's the one who did something wrong? His response comes quickly and the fear becomes worse.

> Professor Olson: By family, do you mean that boyfriend of yours? How will he react when he knows what you've done?

I start typing that I haven't done anything wrong, but a knock on the door startles me. "O-one minute," I squeak past my tight throat.

"Angel," Jake's calm call for me twists my stomach. The only fact that I hear his broken voice reminds me why I can't involve him right now. I remember when it was a smooth baritone. Until he ended up fighting my criminal of a brother and was practically strangled to death. The permanent damage to his vocal cords gives him a hoarse quality that is a constant reminder of our harmful past. I will not be bringing him down with me this time.

"Angel," he repeats, his knuckles rasping on the door. "Are you okay?"

I open the tap to pretend I'm watching my hands and then open the door. His worried gaze scans over me. "Sam said you looked unwell."

I shake my head. "I'm fine. I feel a bit sick. Just stress, I guess."

He nods then reaches for me and grabs my hand. "Everything is gonna be okay. You're turning twenty-two in a few hours. Just enjoy yourself for the night. You can worry about the future tomorrow."

I force a smile on my face just before my phone rings. I glance at Olson's name on my screen and lie straight to my boyfriend's face. "It's my mom. I should take it."

The lie tastes bitter on my tongue, but I escape the bathroom and run up the stairs to the guest bedroom we use when we visit.

Closing the door behind me, I pick up and talk right away. "What do you want?" I panic. "Y-you can't call me..."

"*Are you scared your boyfriend is going to catch you sneaking out to talk to me?*"

"Please," I shake my head. "I'm sorry if there was a misunderstanding. I'm not...I'm not interested in you. I—"

"*No?*" he chuckles coldly. "*Do you think I'm stupid?*" This time the darkness scares me. "*How many of your professors' numbers do you have in your phone, Jamie? You've followed me around like a little puppy for four years. You've spent more time in my office than with your boyfriend. Don't act all innocent now.*"

"I..." I struggle to take a breath as reality hits me. He truly thinks I was coming on to him.

"*You can't act like a little tease for years and then pretend nothing happened,*" he snarls into the phone. "*You've led me on because you thought you could use me to get into med school. Now, it's time to pay up. I can ruin your future. Not only for our college but for any other school you apply to.*"

I shake my head. "No, please." A sob rises in my throat, and I choke swallowing it back down. What if he's right? What if I've been leading him on all along because I thought he could help me get into med...*no*. I didn't do anything wrong.

"*What underwear are you wearing, Jamie?*"

"Stop," I hiss under my breath.

"*Is it the same lacy little thing you were wearing under your dress earlier?*"

"Please, stop." I fall onto the bed behind me, not knowing what to do.

"*Check your phone. I sent you a picture of the email I can easily send to our faculty.*"

My heart is painfully beating against my ribs when I lower the phone in front of me to see the picture of an email to the faculty and dean. He tells them how unprofessional of me it was to attempt to kiss him and offer sexual favors to move up the wait list.

"Don't," I whimper. "You...I didn't..."

"*I think you did,*" he says casually. "*And if you want it to stay between us, all you have to do is play a little game with me. I won't harm you. I promise. Just amuse me, Jamie.*"

"Think of your wife," I plead pitifully. Cold sweat is sending shivers down my back, and I can feel the pressure behind my eyes as tears build up.

"*Don't bring the bitch into this,*" he hisses. "*Now answer. Is it the same flimsy piece of black lace you were wearing earlier? I saw it when you fell off the chair earlier. It made my cock so hard, Jamie.*"

"Please, I need to hang up."

"*Hang up and I'm sending that email right fucking now. You'd be kicked out of college before you even graduate. Now answer me. Is it the same as earlier or not?*"

I shake my head, incapable of coming to terms with the current reality. A sob escapes my tight lips. "No..."

"*Aw, I really liked those ones,*" he mocks me. "*What color are the new ones?*"

"Please, Professor Olson…stop this. I'm begging you." My free hand is gripping the bed cover I'm sitting on and I twist it painfully around my fingers.

"*Just answer the question, pretty girl.*" His dark voice is back again, chilling me to the core.

"Th-they're…w-white," I say with a trembling voice as I cry silently. I'm looking down at my dress barely coming mid-thigh. Is that what I do? Am I a tease who tempted her professor into harassing her?

"*Mm,*" he breathes hard into the phone. "*I'm touching myself thinking about you in your underwear.*" A noise is heard somewhere around him and he huffs. "*My wife needs me,*" he says in a disappointed voice. "*I'll call you back later. Just behave in the meantime.*" There's a short pause. "*And, Jamie, this stays between us or your dreams of becoming a neurosurgeon will be a distant memory when I'm done with you. Got it?*"

"Yes," I whimper.

"*Good. You may go back to your boyfriend now.*"

He hangs up and I squeeze my eyes tightly, hoping when I open them I will wake up from this nightmare.

I don't. Instead, I have to pick up my make-up case in my travel bag and head to the ensuite. My mind goes completely blank as I wash my red face, and redo my gold makeup that makes my green eyes pop. I smile at myself in the mirror pretending everything is okay, and I walk back downstairs to join everyone else.

# 4

## JAMIE

*Battle Scars - MOD SUN*

I don't hear anything else from Olson for the whole rest of the meal. By the time we're done with dessert, alcohol is flowing, and everyone is jolly. I could barely eat anything and every time I tried to take a sip of champagne, my stomach refused to keep still.

"What about you, Jamie?" Lik asks, his handsome smile lighting up as he locks his chocolate eyes on me.

He plays with the golden ring in his nostril as he waits for my answer. I look around, pretty sure I blacked out for the last half hour.

I'm sitting on a sofa with Lik, Sam, Chris, and Rose. I don't even remember when I moved from the dining table to here. Most of the others are outside, smoking joints or getting some fresh air. The window is open to let some of the cold air in, and I can hear them laughing in the backyard from here.

"Sorry, what was the question?" I smile politely, embarrassed that I haven't followed one second of the conversation.

"Chris was just telling us he's going to join Yale law school. What about you? Did you hear back from any med schools?"

My chest is so tight I can't find my breath to reply. Lik must notice how pale I look because he puts a hand on my leg. "You don't have to talk about it," his honey voice reassures me.

He turns back to the rest of the group and nudges Rose. "I told her to apply to Yale too," he says to Chris.

"I'm not applying to Yale," Rose mumbles back like it's a conversation they have often.

"Why not?" Chris asks. "We could be at law school together, just one year apart."

"Because if I apply, I'll get it and then these two," she points at Lik then Sam, "will force me to go. I don't want to go."

"You're applying," Sam states without hesitation.

"You can apply if you're so desperate. I'm happy at SFU," she fights him back. She pours herself another tumbler of whiskey and reaches over Sam's extended legs to grab the ice bucket on the other side of the table. She drops one in her glass, the sloshing sound captivating me. I'm feeling hypersensitive to everything. Particularly my uneven heartbeat.

"I can't believe you left Duke to transfer to Silver Falls University." Chris shakes his head as he gives her a disapproving look.

"They're better than Duke," she throws back at him. "And they're practically begging me to stay for law school."

"She didn't like being away from us." Lik nods to himself and then adds, "And there's the uniform." He bites his lower lip. "I do love the uniform, princess." Lik gets lost in his fantasy of his girlfriend wearing the SFU uniform and ignores us as he relaxes against the sofa.

They're the only college I have ever heard of in the U.S. who has uniforms. They love being the elite of the elite, and most people there come from Stoneview Prep. They're affiliated with them and are basically a continuation of our prep school. I wouldn't be surprised if Rose hates everyone there. But it's one of the best, and it's close to the people she loves.

Sam rolls his eyes and slides his arm behind Rose before poking Lik on the side of the head. "They don't have the uniforms in postgraduate studies."

"What?!" Lik snaps up, turning to Rose.

"Trust me," Sam chuckles. "I checked." His heated gaze runs along Rose's long legs and then goes back to Lik. "They don't have them."

Lik runs his tongue against his teeth before shaking his head disappointedly at his girlfriend. "You said they had the uniforms. That's why I supported your choice."

"Oops," she smiles behind her glass of whiskey. "I must have gotten it wrong." She shrugs and takes another sip.

"Okay," Chris jumps back in, putting us back on topic. "SFU might be better than Duke, but their law school doesn't compare to Yale, Rose," he insists.

"She'll apply to Yale," Sam tells Chris. "I'll make sure of it."

"I'm right here. I can speak for myself," Rose says, annoyed. "And I'll go to SFU."

"With your best friend, Camila," Chris snorts. His hard jaw twists into a taunting smile and he grabs his own glass. I can see the alcohol shining in his amber eyes.

"I already see her all the time. Believe me, she's hard to miss."

"And I'm sure you love it," her foster brother adds before messing her hair. The way Sam tenses isn't missed on me, his knuckles coming to graze his jaw as his dark gaze goes to Chris. "You should definitely stay there then."

Rose gets up and downs her glass of whiskey. "I'm officially bored with this conversation," she says as she steps away to join the others outside.

"She can't take people caring about her," Chris huffs.

"Don't worry," Lik smiles. "We can convince her."

The conversation keeps going, but I can't focus because my phone beeps in my hand. Sam notices at the same time as I do. My brows furrow, my stomach sinking. Why is he so damn observant?

I stand up and go to a different side of the room to check the text I know is from Olson.

> Professor Olson: Does the bra match the white panties?

I try my best to keep a straight face but my entire body freezes with disgust. I can hardly breathe when I reply *yes*. I feel sick thinking that I wore this set for Jake tonight and that I'm now blackmailed into telling Olson about it.

> Professor Olson: Send me a picture.

My eyes widen, my brows shooting to my hairline. My brain refusing to believe what I'm seeing. No. I can't do this.

Pushed into a corner, I go back on my earlier decision. This has gone too far. I don't know if I'm going to regret this, but I need to tell Jake. Olson can't get in the way of our relationship. We've been through enough together and not communicating would only make it worse.

I leave the living room and join the rest of the party

## Chapter 4

outside. Sam has gone outside too, I can see him talking to Jake next to the pool house.

Not caring if I'm going to interrupt an important conversation, I hurry to my boyfriend before stopping dead in my tracks. My eyes glued to my phone.

> Professor Olson: You've got three minutes. Tick-tock. What will your boyfriend think, Jamie? When the scandal comes out that his girlfriend was seducing her professor to get into med school?

I press my lips together to stop the whimper from escaping me. Turning around, I run back inside the house and up the stairs. I close the door to our bedroom and look around, panicking.

*I can't. I can't. I can't do this.*

> Jamie: Give me a minute, please.

> Professor Olson: You've got two left.

My racing heart seems to stop. I'm dying from fear. I stumble back, hitting the wall behind me, and staring at my phone at a total loss.

> Professor Olson: One. Someone wants to be punished.

Fear grabs a tight hold on me and I bring my trembling hands to the spaghetti straps. I free my arms from them before reaching for the zipper at the back.

I don't even stop to wonder what I'm doing. I'm in the middle of a storm, my body and my brain tugging different ways. My limbs are shaking and I'm going to be sick if I move too quickly.

I'm about to let go of the dress completely when the door slams open and Jake appears. I shriek from the surprise, and when our gazes cross, I want to die on the spot.

The fury in his eyes almost annihilates me. His hands are in fists by his side and he's shaking from the anger. Panting because he probably ran up the stairs.

How does he know?

"Jake..."

Without a word, he strides toward me, grabs me by the throat and drags me to a desk at the corner of the room. He pushes me against it, and I'm forced to sit on it as he settles between my legs.

"Give me your phone," he seethes. I slap his forearm, not able to breathe, but instead of releasing me, he snatches my phone from me.

As his focus goes to the text messages, his hold slackens but he still doesn't let me go. He's not saying anything. He doesn't need to, his entire being is reeking of rage.

"Let me explain," I panic. I'm trying to keep my unzipped dress close to my chest but I'm shaking too hard, and the silk keeps falling back down.

He puts my phone in his back pocket and his hand moves from my throat to my jaw so he can hold me tightly without killing me. He's pressing so hard I can feel my inner cheeks against my teeth and my lips pouting.

"I came upstairs to prove Sam wrong," he says low, clearly at his breaking point. His eyes have turned into the kind of blue that announces a storm. His face his hard, his dark stubble hiding any of the smooth features he once had. "And here I am finding my girlfriend about to send nudes to her professor."

I try to shake my head, but his bruising grip stops me.

"Jamie," he hisses. "Do I need to remind you that you belong to me?"

He pulls me off the desk so I'm standing and pulls me closer to him, our chests meeting and his boiling heat burning me. He turns my head to the side, leaning down so he can talk in my ear.

"You are never seeing someone else. You are never leaving me. I will fucking keep you locked in the apartment if needed but there is not one chance in hell, heaven, or this goddamn planet where I let you move on from me. Is that fucking clear?"

"I wasn't—ow!" He slams me against the side of the desk, my back aching from the hit.

"Did you fuck him?" He forces me to look at him now, his midnight eyes completely black. "Did you *fuck him*, Angel?"

"No!" I cry out, but he doesn't listen. He pushes my dress up and spreads my legs further apart.

"Fucking white panties, huh?" He rips them off, making me cry out in panic and looks down between my thighs.

The way his body freezes scares me to death. It's like he couldn't really believe it before, and he's just been proven otherwise. Which is impossible because I did *not* sleep with Olson. Ever.

He lets out a cold chuckle and looks up at me. "Looks like you got bruised when you spread your legs for him."

"I didn't—" He presses into a bruise on my inner thigh, and I look down as I wince.

"No," I panic. I hadn't realised how big the bruises from Olson had gotten. "Jake…" I can't breathe. This is my worst nightmare unfolding right before my eyes. I need to wake up from this. "H-he—" I choke on a sob as Jake pushes me away. I fall backward on the desk.

He takes a step back, grabs my hips and flips me around. "What are you doing?!" I shout as he pushes my dress all the way to my lower back.

I try to straighten back up but he presses a hand between my shoulder blades. "Don't make me hurt you." A second later he lets out a cold laugh and slaps my ass. "Always so fucking wet when she's manhandled. Is that how he got to you too?"

He pushes two fingers inside me from behind, making me cry out and realize how wet I am. The problem with Jake is that my body is completely wired to his way of doing things. Especially to the way he can make fear and pain become so pleasurable.

"Did he bully you into being a little slut for him too?" he mocks me. "You're so desperate for everyone to fucking use you."

His fingers retreat just as I hear his belt unbuckling. "Jake...stop. Listen to me."

I feel his dick pressing at my entrance and my knees almost give up. The hand on my back now comes to grab my neck as he keeps me in place. "Don't talk, Angel. I only want to hear your cries right now." He pushes in harshly and I do exactly what he asked for.

I cry out and he thrusts harder. "You're gonna regret what you did," he hisses. "Because if you think getting caught means I'll let you go, you're so fucking mistaken."

His pace is a punishment, his thrusts only to make a point.

I feel myself getting hotter and wetter but I'm still struggling to try and escape him. "I... didn't...cheat..." I force between my pained moans.

He comes in a rush, not caring whether I'm enjoying myself or not. He pulls out of me and grabs both my hands. I

## Chapter 4

feel him wrapping something around my wrists, but I can't figure out what.

"Stop," I cry out when the material digs into my skin. "You're angry, I understand but..."

"*Angry*?!" he barks. "You've seen nothing, believe me. Those nice panties you were gonna send him look beautiful around your wrists."

He lets me go and I fall to the floor when he takes a step back.

"Stay here," he pants, I gather myself and somehow manage to get back up, but he's already on his way out of the room, grabbing my phone from his jeans.

"What are you doing?" I call as he opens the door. He turns around and points at me.

"You're not going anywhere until I've sorted this out."

"What are you talking about?!"

"You think I'm above locking you up? Don't you fucking know me?"

I take another step, but he slams the door in my face. I hear a click on the other side and look down only to realize he's grabbed the key.

"Jake," I panic. I pull at my binds, but he's wrapped it enough times that it doesn't move even a little bit. "Jake!!" I scream. "You can't just leave me here!"

All I hear are his angry steps as he walks away.

# 5

## JAKE

*lie to me - Tate McRae, Ali Gatie*

Chris's basement is where every single important event has happened for the four of us. This is where Chris deciding to break up with Ella. Of course Luke wasn't there when we had that conversion.

Luke told us he loved Emily in this room—back when he did love her—and it's also here that Ozy admitted she was dating three people at the same time.

This is where I decided to break Jamie's heart senior year to protect her.

Her and I fought past it. We battled through *everything* that has been thrown our way.

I just never thought I'd have to fight her falling out of love with me.

Now, while everyone's significant others are upstairs partying, Luke, Chris, Ozy, and I are standing around the pool table with only one item on it: Jamie's phone.

It's staring back at me, telling me that Sam was right

when he told me she had been on her phone all evening, acting suspicious.

"Okay, are we gonna fucking look at it or what?" Ozy's voice breaks through the tension.

"Jake, this isn't right," Chris says as he runs a hand against his face. "You're not the kind of guy who goes through his girlfriend's phone. You should be talking to her."

"Please," Ozy snorts. "He's exactly that kind of guy. He bullied the girl into loving him for fuck's sake. Going through her phone is foreplay to him."

"Shut the fuck up," I seethe as I point an accusing finger at her. "You're a cheater, a liar, and a bitch. It took three fucking people to keep you in check so don't think I'm gonna listen to anything that comes out of your mouth."

She rolls her eyes at me. "Fine. Go through your girlfriend's phone and see what it does to your relationship."

"I already read most of the texts." I run a hand through my messy hair, ready to pull every single one off my head. "I caught her red-handed about to send a nude to him."

"What?!" they all choke out at the same time.

"This sounds nothing like Jamie," Luke defends.

There's a pause as we all think hard about his words. Even he isn't sure about what he just said.

After a long silence, I'm the one who voices what we all think. "She kissed me when she was with Nate."

"That was a different time and a very complicated situation," Luke continues with little conviction.

"Your brother was the biggest liar in that case. He manipulated and used her. She wanted you," Chris reassures me.

"And now she wants her Biochem professor." My legs

give up and I end up sitting on the back of the sofa behind me.

I run a hand over my face, not able to process this is actually happening.

"Alright, that's it. I'm fucking looking," Ozy huffs as she grabs the phone. They all huddle up around her. "Password."

"1031," I whisper, completely dejected. Anxiety is eating me from the inside.

"Aw, my birthday," she smiles.

"*My* birthday," I correct her, getting hung up on the tiny things that tell me Jamie loves me.

"Tomato, to-mah-to. I guess we'll never know who it was really for."

"You're pissing me off and I have zero patience for you right now."

She ignores me as I'm assuming she's scrolling through Jamie's texts.

"What the fuck?" Luke murmurs, his eyes on the screen. "She came on to him?"

"That can't be true," Ozy adds, not really believing her own words when everything is right in front of her.

"How does he know the color of her underwear, then?" Luke asks.

While they all focus on the phone, I dig into my pocket and put something on the pool table.

"There must be a misunderstanding," Chris finally lets out. "You said you caught her about to send him the picture he asked for?"

They all look back at me, catch what's on the table, and freeze.

"Shit," Ozy drops.

"Jake..." The pity in Chris's voice breaks my heart.

## Chapter 5

Luke takes a deep breath, looking sorry for me. "When were you going to ask?"

I grab the small box on the table and open it before putting it back. We all stare at the engagement ring and a cold sadness takes over the room.

"At seven thirty-one a.m. That's when she was born."

"You need to talk to her," Chris repeats. "You can't just give everything up when you haven't even talked to her. You have to hear her side."

"I can't talk to her right now," I shake my head, my throat tightening.

"Jakey, come on. Communication is key in any relationship. And that's coming from *me*."

"I can't," I repeat. "I'm not calm. I'll hurt her." I inhale through my nose, trying to still my racing heart in vain. "I can't fucking look at her," I push past gritted teeth.

"Where is she?" Luke asks.

"Upstairs, in our bedroom."

"She's probably looking for you," Chris says as he puts a hand on my shoulder.

"She's locked in."

"What?!" My friend lets go of me and takes a step back. "You fucking locked her in the room?"

"That sounds more like you," Ozy nods to herself.

"Tied her up too," I mumble, not proud of myself but knowing I wouldn't do it any other way.

"Fucking hell." Luke huffs as he sits down next to me. "And here we thought Chris and Megan were bad."

I'm so wrapped in anxiety I feel like I'm going to be sick. I'm cold, my hands trembling and my chest tight.

"What if she leaves me?" I push past my tight throat.

"Tying her up and locking her in your room won't change that! You can't kidnap her because she *might* have cheated on you," Chris scolds me. "Jake, that's not how relationships work. I'm not saying she does, but if Jamie did want to leave you, you'd have to let her go. Even if she does it in the worst way possible and cheats on you."

"I'm not letting her go," I shake my head. "Not in this lifetime."

"You don't even want to talk to her. Act like an adult, for fuck's sake." Chris was the first one to be friends with Jamie back then. He was always protective over her. "This thread of messages might sound like she did something wrong but you saw how anxious she was all night. And that picture of the email makes it sound like a threat. What if she's done nothing wrong? What if he's blackmailing her?"

"Doesn't look like blackmail to me," I fight back. I stand up, facing him as my anxiety translates into fury. "Sounds to me like she wants to move up the wait list. Med school is her dream and she'll stop at nothing to get it. I fucking know that. Everyone knows that. What's sleeping with your professor when you could get into your dream school?" I'm panting, chest to chest with my foster brother.

"You're being angry and delusional," Ozy adds softly as she puts a hand on my arm, pulling me away from Chris. "Come on, you have to calm down before you do something you regret."

"I don't fucking care what I'm being. She's not getting out. And he's dead."

"Wow, you sound realistic as fuck. As usual," Ozy mocks me.

I turn to my sister, showing her how furious she's making me. "I'm gonna p—"

"He's blackmailing her." Luke's voice cuts through our argument. He's got the phone in his hand and shows me the screen.

## Chapter 5

He sent a message pretending to be Jamie.

> Jamie: What are you going to do if I don't send it?

Professor Olson: Maybe you're not scared about the faculty. How about we change our game. Should I contact your boyfriend? How will he react when he learns you're talking to me about your beautiful underwear?

"That means nothing..." I state, finding it difficult to get out of my own head.

"He called her earlier tonight. Probably because he didn't want to put his threats in text. I know how you read the conversation, Jake. But try again, imagine that at some point he called her to threaten her then read it again."

I do. I grab the phone and reread the whole thing from a different perspective. The way she tried to ignore him and pleaded to talk about it another time.

Two *please's* asking to talk about it later? That's leave me the fuck alone in Jamie's language.

And the picture of the email. Of course that's a threat.

She looked so unwell tonight but I thought it was because of the rejection letter she received this morning.

"He's blackmailing her," I huff out. Jamie might not be cheating on me, but the anxiety and anger don't go away. "He..." I chuckle, feeling myself falling into insanity. "He blackmailed my girlfriend into sending him pictures of her in her underwear."

My three best friends are looking at me like I've lost it. I think I have.

"You should go talk to Jamie. At least unlock the damn door and untie her," Chris says softly.

"Oh no," I shake my head. "Absolutely not."

"Are you fucking dumb?" Ozy snaps. "If you don't let her out, I will."

"No one is letting her out."

"For god's sake, why?" Luke says as he puts the phone down.

I smile at my best friends as I let common sense escape my body slowly, replaced by electric insanity.

"Because we're going to find the guy and we're going to make him regret even looking at my girl. And if Jamie gets out of that room, she's going to stop us."

"Jake," Chris sighs.

We all look at each other, and I feel the moment they shift and understand I'm not backing out of this.

"Alright," Ozy shrugs. "Let's fucking do it." Of course, she's my ride or die. Any stupid shit I want to do, she's got my back.

"He won't understand what's coming for him." Luke nods sternly.

We turn to Chris, waiting for the only wise one in our group to give us the go ahead. I can see right and wrong battling in his eyes. Eventually, his Superman complex takes over. "Let's find him."

They're simple words, but to our group it means everything when calm and collected Chris Murray has our backs.

I grab the phone and turn to them. "We could drive to there tonight. Make him meet us somewhere. It's only a four-hour drive at this time."

Ozy scoffs. "Four hours there, four hours back, who knows how many hours torturing the asshole. Do you think

## Chapter 5

I can disappear for that long without having Sam, Lik, and Rach declaring me missing?"

"You used to disappear on us all the time," I snap back.

"Not to hurt your feelings, but you're not nearly as scary as Sam and I don't care when you're mad at me."

"Thanks for absolutely nothing," I mumble as I unlock the phone again.

"We could just make him come here," Chris suggests. "Lure him in, take care of him. He can bring himself back home and that will save us time."

"That sounds better," Ozy nods.

"How are we gonna get the guy to drive all the way to Stoneview?"

Luke snaps the phone from my hands. "Well, sorry to say, but he clearly has it for Jamie. Stupidly so. I'm sure he'll meet her anywhere."

My hands tighten into fists by my side as Luke taps on the phone and sends a text. I want to step on Olson's fucking throat. The man is going to remember the exact moment he decided to blackmail my queen. And he will regret it forever.

> Jamie: There's a reason I didn't send the picture. I've been thinking and I want to take you up on your offer. Meet me and I'll give you anything you want. As long as it takes me to med school.

There's a sickness growing inside me that threatens to kill me when the fucker answers.

> Professor Olson: Someone's finally understanding what I can do for her. Anything?

"I can't fucking watch this," I spit as I turn away and walk to the other side of the room.

I'm running my hands through my hair, pulling at the roots, and driving myself insane when Luke finally says. "He's coming."

"Here?"

"Here," he nods. "Two a.m."

My heart drops to my stomach and adrenaline fires up my blood. I smile at my friends. "Dead man incoming."

# 6

## JAKE

*Love Runs Out - Marting Garrix, G-Eazy, Sasha Alex Sloan*

It's not easy to go back upstairs and pretend like everything is normal. When Emily asks where Jamie is, I tell her she wasn't feeling well and fell asleep. That the stress of med school is really getting to her. At midnight, I check on her. She managed to get in bed and fell asleep.

My heart breaks watching the wetness on the pillow from her tears. She's sleeping on her side so she's not crushing her arms tied at her back. I sit down next to her and kiss her cheek then her neck, nipping at her soft skin.

She lets out a contented sigh and I keep going.

Sliding closer to her, I wrap a hand around her waist and go from her neck to her naked shoulder. She's not been able to put her dress properly back on since her wrists are tied.

My hand drops to between her thighs and I cup her sex under her silk dress. Her legs part automatically and she lets out another sigh. This one sounds a lot more like a soft moan.

Jamie and I have a lot of practice with somnophilia.

She loves being woken up with pleasure and it turns me on to know I have total control over her body. I'm not mad at her like I was earlier, blinded by the rage, but I still want to claim my girl back. The simple fact that Olson thought he could force her to talk about her underwear, that he could blackmail her into sending pictures...My hand presses harder against her sex and her hips buck, pushing back against me. She's so deeply asleep I don't think she realizes what she's doing. Even less that she's getting wet.

I start playing with her clit. Slow languid circles that make her shiver from pleasure.

I keep the same pace, torturing her sleeping body with a teasing touch that can't quite give her what she wants. I feel myself getting hard and I grind my erection against her ass. Her breathing accelerates and another moan escapes her.

My fingers leave her clit and lower to her entrance. My erection becomes painful and I push harder against her. As soon as I push the tip of my finger through her wet entrance, she shifts.

"Jake," she moans as she grinds against my hand.

"Shh." I kiss her neck again. "Keep sleeping, Angel."

She's sleeping anyway, not aware that she's talking and that her body is encouraging my hand to keep fucking her. I insert another finger and fuck her slowly, grazing her g-spot and watching her tremble.

I do it over and over again, until she's whimpering in her sleep and trying to move from the position I'm keeping her in.

"Are you going to come in your sleep?" I murmur against her ear. "My good little slut coming apart for me whenever I want her to?"

There's a low mumble before her panting accelerates. I

## Chapter 6

keep going excruciatingly slow and her little cries electrify my body.

"Your body belongs to me, Angel. Let go and give me what I want."

For a split second she freezes, before exploding against my fingers. She bucks and writhes, her body at a complete loss of control.

When I finally pull away, she sags against the bed.

"More," I hear in a low sigh. She's starting to wake up, halfway between dream and reality. I watch as she shifts and gathers the covers between her legs. "More," she whimpers. Is she dreaming? Wrapping her legs around the bundle of covers, she starts grinding against it.

"Shit," I groan as I grab my hard cock through my pants. "Jamie, you're so hot."

The only response I get is a low grunt of frustration as she keeps grinding her needy pussy against the covers.

I go to her bag and grab her sneakers, pulling the laces out of them. Coming back to the bed, I grab her ankles and tie them together. That finally brings her out of the sleeping realm.

"Jake?" she croaks.

"Hello, baby."

She hisses when I tighten the laces around her ankle. "What are you doing?" she panics.

"Shh. Don't be scared. You know I'm not going to hurt you."

"I didn't do anything," she whimpers. "I promise you." Her voice is barely a rasp from her sleep. "Please, you have to believe me. It was him he—"

"I know, baby. I know."

"You know? You believe me?"

Instead of answering, I grab my belt and undo it before

wrapping it around her thighs.

"If-if you know the truth, then what are you doing?" She tries to twist away as I buckle my belt tightly against her thighs, keeping her legs firmly shut.

"Because my little slut isn't getting out yet. And I'll be damned if I let her make herself come against the sheets while I'm away."

"Jake," she sighs. "What do you mean by away? Untie me, we need to talk about this."

"I'm just going to have fun with everyone downstairs and it makes me fucking hard to know you're here, all wet and needy, and can't do anything about it. All you can do is desperately wait for me to come and make you feel good."

I push a finger past her slit and rub her clit just before pulling away. She moans as her eyes close again.

"Don't leave me here. Please."

"It's for your own sake. Be a good girl and go back to sleep." I give her a deep kiss. Our own way of reassuring the other. "Happy new year, Angel."

I don't say happy birthday because we like keeping the two separate. Midnight is for the new year, morning is for Jamie.

And when I come back tomorrow morning, my future wife will be safe from the man who tried to hurt her.

"Open," I tell Chris as we watch Olson's car stopping right in front of the gates through the video link on his phone.

Ozy opens the door to the basement and runs down the stairs. "You have to get him in through the back. Everyone has gone to bed but Lik and Sam. They're still being two lovebirds in the living room."

I take a deep breath and huff it out. "Alright."

## Chapter 6

We watch Olson park in the driveway and when I walk up the stairs, I take the door that leads directly to the garage. I send a text with Jamie's phone, telling Olson to come to the garage and knock once. As soon as I hear him, I cross the room that can fit about ten cars and walk out through the door on the other side.

"Hello professor Olson," I smile calmly.

"What—" My fist to his chin shuts him up real quick. In fact, it knocks him out right away.

I drag him into the garage and get Chris to help me bring him down.

We tie him to a chair, and all sit on the sofa as we wait for him to wake up. "I hope this doesn't last too long," Luke yawns. "I do want to go to bed at some point."

"You're such an old man," Rose laughs.

"I'm a CEO. That shit takes energy out of you, I'm telling you."

"Oh, I'm sorry, Mr. Baker," she mocks him. "Please don't fire me."

I want to take part in the fun but I physically can't. My eyes are trained on Olson, waiting for him to wake up just so I can hurt him.

It doesn't take long before he startles, looking around and panicking as he pulls at his binds.

"Welcome back," I tell him low.

"Wh-who are you?" he panics. "You four are in big fucking trouble, I'm telling you. You have no idea who I am. Who put you up to this, huh? Was it that little slut, Jamie?"

I'm on him in a split second, punching the lights out of him.

"Jake, man!" Ozy complains. "He'd just woken up. Now we have to wait all over again."

"Maybe he'll think twice before he calls Jamie a slut," I

growl as I fall back on the sofa.

"I'll do the talking next time he wakes up," Chris tells me calmly. "You just try to keep your fists to yourself."

"Tsk, tsk. This boy is so violent," Rose pretends to be disappointed in me like I'm a problematic kid.

I turn to her and raise an eyebrow at her. "I would love to see your reaction if anything like that had happened to Rachel."

"Please," she snorts. "The last time someone hurt my fiancée, I choked him unconscious and helped her stab him. What you're doing is child's play."

"This is not something to be proud of, Rose," Chris scolds her.

She stretches her arms on the back of the sofa. "I'm very proud." She smiles up at him just as Olson wakes up again.

"What the...what the..." he panics.

"Think twice before you call my girl a slut," I say to him as I get up and tower over him. "You haven't exactly put me in a good mood tonight."

He looks at me then the others. "I didn't do anything wrong. I swear I didn't."

"No? Did she blackmail herself into sending you pictures of her?"

"You have to understand." He pulls at his binds and looks into my eyes. "She came on to me! She's the one who came to my office. The things she said to me, you wouldn't even believe me. She wants that space in med school. She'd do anything for it."

"Motherf—" I try to jump him again, but this time Luke and Chris hold me back.

They pull me away from him and Chris takes my space right in front of the chair.

"Here's what's going to happen," he says with the calm of

## Chapter 6

someone who is ready to kill Olson with his bare hands. "You're going to confess what you did on video so we know you can't blackmail her. Apologize to Jamie and leave her alone. On Monday you're going to resign from your post and never teach again."

He leans toward him, bringing his face right in front of Olson's. "You will never hurt another girl again, understand? And if you don't leave Jamie alone, there will be nothing and no one that will protect you from us. Am I making myself clear?"

There's a pause before Olson shakes his head. "You're mistaken. She came onto me. I won't lose my entire life and career because the girl was willing to suck dick for a place in med school."

I'm going to kill the motherfucker. I stand up, but Ozy is already there. She pushes Chris out the way and in one swift movement, she crushes her foot on Olson's crotch so hard the chair falls backward.

We all wince in unison as Olson screams. He crashes on the floor and hits his head, his eyes rolling to the back of their sockets before he comes back to us. Ozy pulls out a cigarette and lights it up before inhaling deeply. Probably trying to calm herself down.

"I must warn you," she says as she looks down at him. "I've got no patience for predators. So if you think blackmailing a girl into sexual assault and blaming her for it is going to run with us, I say think again. What do you say, Jake. Is it time to cut his balls off yet?"

I sense Chris wanting to stop Ozy and I, but I don't let him. I join my twin, standing on the other side of Olson.

"I say first we're going to get a confession out of him. And if he doesn't cooperate then we get to the balls."

"Mm, great idea," she nods. "We'll start like this." She

takes a drag out of her cigarette. "But if you don't cooperate, you might be missing a few teeth by the time you want to confess."

His body starts to shake but he moves his head from side to side. "I didn't do anything wrong. Please...I didn't."

"Lying isn't going to get you anywhere," Chris adds.

"Look," Luke says as he steps closer as well. "Us two," he points at Chris then himself, "we're the good guys. These two," he points at Ozy and me, "they're fucking insane. We'll try to hold them back as much as we can, but we can't be on your side if you don't help us, Olson. Do it the easy way, man, just confess and disappear." He lets out an exaggerated huff. "I mean, I don't even want to know how far these two will go if we let them run free."

"Could kill him," Ozy mumbles around her cigarette. "Can't hurt anyone then, can he?"

"I didn't...I-I...please."

"Right," I nod. I grab his glasses off his face and put them to the side. "You had your chance." Without any other warning, my foot comes crashing on his face. I feel his nose crack under my shoe.

"Help!" he screams, and we all pause.

*Shit*. Lik and Sam are still upstairs.

Rose suddenly takes her sweater off. She shoves her entire sleeve into Olson's mouth and puts her index finger to her mouth. "Shh. I promise you, you don't want my boyfriends to come down. I'm gonna be in trouble, but you...oh boy, you'll wish you'd just dealt with us."

After three rounds of beating him up for a confession, and even Chris taking his turn, I've had enough.

"I'm fucking done," I say as I wipe my forehead. My knuckles are busted and I've no fucking energy to spend on him when my girl is waiting for me upstairs.

## Chapter 6

I grab the chair and put it back on its feet. Looking around the room, an idea comes to me. I go to the closet where I know the Murrays keep their tools, grab a toolbox, and take a screwdriver out of it.

"And you're done too," I tell Olson. I stride back to him, squat and without a second thought, I stab him in the stomach. "Listen to me, asshole," I seethe as he screams into his gag. "Let's try this one more time. We're going to take the gag out, we're going to film your confession, then you're gonna go home and disappear off the face of the earth. Am I making myself fucking clear?"

For the first time tonight, we get a nod. "Atta boy," I smile. I grab my phone as Ozy takes out the gag.

"Undress him," I tell Luke and Chris. They don't question anything. My brothers have my back and they get to it quickly. In less than a minute, his pants and boxers are around his bounded ankles, and his shirt is bunched up around his tied wrists.

Once he's completely naked and crying, I talk to him. "Make sure to state your name and what you did exactly. I want to know where those bruises were from."

"P-please," he babbles as snot runs down his face. "I don't want to die."

"Just get talking," Ozy snaps as she presses her boot exactly where I stabbed him.

I press record on my phone and point it at him.

"M-my name is Jordan Olson." He looks around, crying some more and I make a gesture to keep going. "I'm sorry... I'm sorry, okay? Jamie has been my favorite student for the last four years. I...I don't how it happened. I became obsessed. She's so beautiful, so sweet. She's so small I just want to hold her close. Isn't she the most adorabl—"

"Fucking get to it," I growl. I can't hear this.

"I'm the one who told the board to put her on the wait list. I wanted to use it to blackmail her into being with me. I wanted to play games...I wanted her to be mine."

He cries some more and shakes his head. "Jamie, I'm sorry. Please, I'm in love with you. I'll leave my wife. I don't care that she's having our baby. Jamie, I love you."

"For fuck's sake," Rose huffs. "Jamie isn't going to fucking see this, asshole. Just say what you did."

"I...I invited her to my office and I offered to move her up the wait list and get her into med school."

"The bruises. What did you do?" I ask. My jaw clenches tighter and tighter the more I'm listening, but I need to know everything.

"I grabbed her thigh. It was a little too hard, I couldn't control myself. You don't understand! I've waited for so long to touch her. I'm sorry, Jamie," he cries out. "I didn't want to hurt you. I know I scared you. Oh no," he panics. "She looked so scared. And then I panicked when she pushed me away. I pretended it was her. I told her I'd tell the committee and she'd get kicked out of college. I-I called her and told her to tell me about her underwear...b-but that's only because I love her! That's only because she makes me so fucking hard..."

The phone is out of my hand in a split second, bouncing against Olson's head. Did I throw that? I jump on him, raining punches on his face.

"Stop talking," I seethe. "Stop talking to her, about her... stop fucking *thinking* of her." I don't know how many times I punch him. I only know that when I start choking him, a pair of strong arms pull me away. I'm fighting them, but it must be Chris because he's taller than me and he finally manages to hold me back.

"Calm down."

That's not Chris.

It's a British accent.

"Don't fucking tell me to calm down!" I scream.

Sam brings me with him to a corner of the room, pushing me against the wall. "I'm telling you, calm down."

"You don't know!" I rage. "You don't fucking know what he did...the..." I struggle to catch my breath. "The way he's thinking about her...You have no idea what it's like!!"

"I think I do." Our eyes clash and I look away. Of course he does. He's been through worse.

I run a hand against my face, wiping the sweat. My hands are bloody, my knuckles are killing me. How much did I hit him?

"Don't hold me back, Sam. Let me fucking end him."

He chuckles. "I've spent my entire life holding your brother back so his psychopathic ass wouldn't kill too many people. I'm pretty sure I can do it with you too."

Jaw clenched, I look away knowing he's right. I take a deep breath and nod at him.

"I hope he's still breathing," he tells me with that infamous calm. "Or you'll really have ruined my New Year's Eve."

I sniffle and run my arm under my nose. "I don't give a shit."

He gives me an annoyed look but doesn't say anything else. Probably since he killed enough men because of my sister that he categorizes as a serial killer at this point. He knows he can't really judge me.

He steps away from me and we walk back to where everyone is huddled up around Olson.

"I see you guys have been having fun without us," Lik smiles.

Sam comes to stand on the other side of Rose and puts a possessive hand at the back of her neck.

"It was for a good reason," she mumbles like she got herself in trouble.

"Oh, princess," Lik sighs. "Always with the catastrophic behavior."

Chris bends down and grabs my phone. "The video is all good," he tells all of us.

"Send it to your phone," I say. "We need multiple copies."

"And to his wife," Ozy adds.

I nod, agreeing with her.

Luke squats next to Olson and checks his pulse. The chair has fallen back again after I beat him to a pulp. "He's alive. Disfigured but alive."

Olson groans something and his eyes flutter open. "I just want to go home...please."

"Put him in his car and send him home," Sam tells us. "Remind him that if he goes to the police, you'll hand them the video."

Rose nods. "Okay, we can do that."

"Not you," he tells her sternly. "You're going to bed."

"But—"

"Now."

"Whatever," she mumbles. "You're not even fun."

He drags her with him as they cross the room. "I'll show you fun."

"She's like a fucking kid," Lik tuts as he goes up the stairs with them. "You know when she's been quiet for a while it's because she's doing something terrible."

They disappear into the hallway and I turn back to Olson. "You're so lucky I didn't get you alone. You wouldn't have made it to the second day of this year."

# 7

## JAKE

*Electric Love - BØRNS*

When we've finally gotten rid of Olson, I walk back upstairs. I should take a shower, calm myself down, but I can't. I'm too eager to see Jamie.

I open the door slowly, not sure if she's awake or not. She's fallen asleep again. She must be so uncomfortable. She's facing away from me, and I've got a perfect view of her naked ass, her dress bunched up at her hips and her hands tied behind her back. I walk to her and run my hand against her ass before undoing her hands and her legs. She rolls onto her back and her eyes open slowly.

"Jake..." she says in a groggy voice. "Where have you been?"

Instead of answering I spread her legs and place myself between them. I lower my head and kiss her inner thighs. "You've been so good to me, Jamie." I kiss her closer to her slit. "So perfect." Another kiss closer. "I don't deserve you. I don't deserve the goddess you are." I kiss just above her clit and she trembles. "I know why you didn't say anything. You didn't want to cause trouble."

She goes on her elbows and looks down at me. "What happened?" The fear in her voice tells me she knows I was up to no good. She's scared for me.

I look up at her. "I will always protect you, Angel. Don't you know that? Even when you don't want me to. Even when you think you can protect yourself. I'll always be there, chasing your demons like you chased mine."

"Jake..."

I don't let her talk. I thrust my tongue into her perfect pussy, and she falls back against the pillows. I lick her from her entrance to her clit and slowly stroke it with a flat tongue.

"Oh gosh," she cries out. Her hands come to my hair, pulling at the strands as she pushes against my mouth.

"Baby, you are so perfectly mine," I whisper against her sensitive clit. I go back to licking and nipping. I drive her insane before finally bringing her to orgasm. I relish in the way her thighs close around my head and she screams into the dead of the night.

I come up and kiss her, forcing her to taste herself. She opens her mouth for me, stroking my tongue and giving me all of herself.

I pull away and get rid of my jeans and t-shirt. I pull her dress down and get rid of her bra so I can access her tits.

Aligning myself with her, I take my time teasing her before pushing in slowly. She moans and trembles, her legs wrapping around my waist as I go further. My hands come to her boobs and I grab them. Her eyes drop and widen when she sees my busted knuckles.

"What have you done?" she pants. "Jake what—"

"I won't let anyone hurt you, do you understand?" I

thrust inside her, and her mouth falls open. "No one." Thrust. "Hurts." Thrust. "You." I roll my hips and drink her moans when I hit her g-spot. I go back on my legs slightly and angle myself perfectly to keep hitting it. Her hips lift, following the pleasure. I fuck her like I'm insane. Like the kind of man who would beat up someone to an inch of their life if they dare upset her.

She tightens around my dick when she comes, moaning my name like I'm her favorite dream and her worst nightmare all at the same time.

And I take it all in because that's exactly what I am.

Blinding pleasure zaps through my entire body as I come inside her. I fall on top of her and push her hair away from her face. "I love you, Angel."

"I love you," she smiles. "But I am furious at you, obviously."

I shrug and give her my brightest smile. "I can live with that." My head falls in the crook of her neck and I crush her under my weight.

"Can't breathe," she rasps.

"Just one more second," I sigh lovingly, wrapping my arms tightly around her.

*Jamie*

I'm alone when I wake up. I have no idea of the time and I automatically look at the digital clock on the bedside table. Seven a.m. I notice my phone right next to it and roll over to grab it. I unlock it and anxiety grips me, cold and deadly.

I haven't heard from Olson.

I check our conversation and notice texts I don't

remember sending. Inviting him to Chris's? Asking him to come to the garage?

I sit up, foggy from sleep and not sure if anything is real or not. I rub my eyes, look around the room, and check my phone again.

*Jake.*

It must have been him.

Everything comes back slowly. I was practically asleep but I remember when he came in the room the first time. He tied me up further and left me here. And then he returned and said everything was taken care of.

*He killed him. He must have killed him.*

"I didn't kill him." My boyfriend's raspy voice startles me.

"Your thoughts are so loud I can hear them, Angel. I didn't kill him. I just hurt him very badly. Taught him a well needed lesson, that's all."

I watch him with wide eyes as he approaches me. He's holding a glass of water and an envelope. It's the morning, and there's one thing Jake hates when he wakes up; wearing a shirt. His beautiful, tanned body is on display for me. For a second the entire world stops spinning as I take in his wide shoulders, defined abs, and the Adonis belt that makes me weak at the knees. He's wearing a pair of gray sweats and I completely lose focus when my eyes catch the outline of his dick.

"Someone still isn't satiated," he chuckles playfully.

I shake my head, trying to refocus. "He could sue you. Blackmail you. Who knows."

"Nah," he shakes his head and smiles at me. "I've got his confession on my phone, and so does his wife. I can safely tell you that everything is fine."

"I'm not fine," I tell him sternly. "I don't want you to get yourself in trouble for me. I don't like knowing something bad could happen to you and it's all my fault."

"But I'm supposed to stand by and let him blackmail you into doing whatever he wants? Do you think he would have stopped at pictures of you in underwear, Jamie? He wouldn't even have stopped at a picture of you completely naked."

I shift uncomfortably under the covers, pressing my back to the headboard.

"I...I would have figured something out. Gone to the police."

"You don't exactly have a record of going to the police when a man does something wrong to you."

I bite my inner cheek. We both know he's talking about himself.

"That was different. I would have fought Olson back."

"We found ropes, gags, sex toys, and some stuff I don't even want to tell you about in his car. Jamie, if he'd gotten his hands on you, he would have never let you go."

My stomach twists and for a second I'm sure I'm going to be sick on the bed. "He's crazy," I rasp.

"Yeah. I always thought he was too flirty with you. But he was fucking obsessed on a level I couldn't even have imagined."

"Please, Jake. Promise me you didn't kill him. I know this angered you but if you killed him then he's the victim and you're going to prison when they find his body."

"I didn't kill him, Jamie. I cut his dick off and sent him home with it on his passenger seat. But I didn't kill him. Not because I didn't want to and not because that would make him a victim. I didn't kill him because Sam stopped me. And when I had a second to think clearly, I realized I didn't want to do something that would upset you, or worse, make you afraid of me."

I feel like I've been afraid of Jake so many times in high school, I'm not sure I could survive it again.

"Thank you," I whisper as he puts the glass of water and envelope on the bedside table. I crawl across the bed, go on my knees and put my arms around his neck before kissing him. The infinite, unconditional love I have for him is impossible to put into words, so I try to give it to him through our kiss. He must have showered earlier because he smells fresh and comfortable.

When we pull apart, he puts a strand of my brown hair behind my ear and kisses the tip of my nose.

"I have something for you," he tells me with a smile tipping at the corner of his mouth.

"Oh?" I cock my head to the side. He grabs the envelope and shows it to me.

The Silver Falls University blazon is stamped on it.

My ass falls back on the bed. "Oh my gosh." With everything that happened yesterday after I opened my rejection letter from Grossman, I forgot I had an envelope from SFU. Olson occupied my mind so much that I didn't even think that I still had a chance to fulfill my dream.

"Give it to me," I order as I straighten back up.

"Ah, ah," he smiles as he raises it high above his head. "You, young lady, are going to have a shower and rehydrate before you get to open this letter."

"Jake!" I bark, as I stand on the bed. "Give me the damn envelope. And I'm older than you!"

It doesn't take him much to wrap one arm around my waist and carry me to the bathroom like a sack of potatoes, the envelope in his other hand.

"I'm going to strangle you!" I fight him. He pushes me in the shower, my dress from yesterday nothing but a band around my hips, and turns the shower on.

## Chapter 7

"It's freezing!" I shriek.

"Shower," he throws back as he exits the bathroom.

I get rid of my dress and shower in record time. Running back into the room with only a towel around me and my hair dripping, I look around. "Where is it?"

"Drink," he orders as he passes me the glass. I take a few small sips and try to give it back to him. "The whole thing, Jamie. None of your baby sips you always try to fool me with." He rolls his eyes at me, and I bring the glass to my lips again. I down it at the speed of light and give it back to him.

"Okay give it to me now!"

He grabs it from his pocket and gives it to me. But once I have it in my hands, I freeze. I fall on the bed and look up at him.

"This is my last chance," I whisper, afraid that it'll be even truer if I say it loudly.

"Angel, it doesn't matter whether you get in or not. You are made for great things and I will support you no matter what happens."

"Easy to say when you dropped out of college and built an app that someone just bought for millions of dollars," I grumble.

He lets out a soft laugh and caresses my head. "Even better. I can take care of you. I'll keep you at home where I know no one can hurt you. A gilded cage for my beautiful girl." His eyes light up with intense flames as his hand tightens in my hair. "Mm, I'll get you pregnant and you'll be my perfect wife."

My eyes widen. Jake has never ever talked about having kids. I want them. I want lots of them. But he always avoids the topic. His own childhood was too messed up for him to ever envision himself as a dad and he's told me that before. His words are not because he wants a family. They're a way of keeping me to himself and for me to have nowhere else to go.

I lick my lips, not because any of this sounds even remotely okay, but because the passion in his voice and the hold on me starts a fire in me. The way he craves to possess me makes me feel a million messed up, dark things. I don't think that will ever change. We will always live in this gray area that makes us an example to never follow. But we're perfect for each other, and I wouldn't change a thing.

His grip turns into a hand cupping the back of my head and he kisses my lips softly. "But I guess you can also go to med school and come back to me every night. For now."

I laugh as I shake my head. "Okay," I say in a trembling voice. Here goes nothing.

I open the envelope and bring it in front of my face, hiding Jake from my view. I can't look at him while I do this. I know he's going to be looking for the answers in my eyes.

This time, I read in my head rather than mumble it like I've done with all the other letters.

"Oh my gosh," I say in a tight voice. Tears prick the back of my eyes but today, I don't let them fall. Why are happy tears always so easy to hold back when they should be the ones running down your face as you celebrate?

"I got in!! Baby, I got in!!" He doesn't say anything so I keep going. Ecstatic, I read from the very top. "Dear Miss Williams, congratulations on your acceptance at Silver Falls University School of Medicine. Your notable accomplishments and enthusiasm for the program stood out to us among a competitive pool of applicants...I got in! Oh my gosh, I'm going to be at SFU with Rose! I got in, I got in. Jake, I got in!"

"I hear you." His voice is deadly calm. Tight even. I lower

the envelope and freeze when I find him on one knee in front of me.

"Congratulations, Angel. And happy birthday."

My eyes dart to the clock. 7:31 a.m.

"What..." There's a small black, velvet box in his hands, and my throat dries out, making it hard to swallow as he opens it and reveals a beautiful engagement ring. "Jake..."

"Jamie." He licks his lips and looks up right into my eyes. His voice is like I've never heard before. His usual confidence and cockiness is crushed by a quiver he can't control. "Exactly twenty-two years ago, fate put an angel on this earth, and I believe she was meant for me. I truly believe I was meant to go through all the hardships life put me through, and you through yours, so that we could cross paths and find happiness, repentance, and respite in each other. The day I realized I was in love with you, I started breathing for the first time. There isn't one day I will spend without you. There isn't one second of one minute I will not love you. Be mine forever, and I will protect you from everything. I will pick you up when you're down and help you fly when you wish to reach higher. Be my wife, Angel, and I promise the world will be ours."

The sob that bursts out of me is a ball of joy I can't hold back any longer.

"Will you marry me?" he insists as I jump on him. We both fall onto the floor, rolling around until I'm straddling him.

"Yes," I cry. "Yes, of course I will marry you."

He grabs my hand and places the shining diamond at the tip of my ring finger.

"Kiss me, baby. Give me one last kiss as my girlfriend before you become my wife."

I crush my lips onto his, our happiness mixing and

bursting fireworks in my stomach. As I do so, he pushes the ring all the way, locking it around my finger and making it all official.

We separate and I straighten up before looking down at my hand.

"My gosh," I sniffle. I grab my wrist, pretending my left hand is heavy. "It's a huge rock. This is a millionaire's ring."

"Your fiancé is a millionaire, what can I say," he shrugs.

He grabs my hips and rolls around so he's the one on top. Then he falls onto me, holding me closely as he crushes me the way he loves.

"My fiancé. I like that." I grin as I run my hands through his messy strands.

"You said yes," he breathes out, the final remnants of his stress escaping his body. "You're marrying me," he says softly in my ear. "No take backs."

"I said yes," I giggle. "You probably would have bullied me into saying yes if I hadn't anyway."

We burst into a laugh, and I wrap my arms around his strong back.

"Probably."

The end

Want to see what Jake and Jamie look like? Sign up to my newsletter for some exclusive content... Click here! Or type https://bit.ly/LolaKingSubscribe in your browser!

# ALSO BY LOLA KING

All books unfold in the same world at different times.

STONVEVIEW STORIES

*Stoneview Trilogy (MF Bully):*

Giving In

Giving Away

Giving Up

One Last Kiss (Novella)

*Rose's Duet (FFMM why-choose):*

Queen Of Broken Hearts (Prequel novella)

King of My Heart

Ace of All Hearts

# ACKNOWLEDGMENTS

Thank you to my readers who have followed Jake and Jamie until now. I am forever grateful.

Thank you to Lauren for always reading my stories and helping make them better.

Thank you to Nikki for handling everything while I write and also while I don't write.

Thank you to my partner for being my anchor. I love you with my entire heart, body, and soul.

Thank you to Jess for the motivation, the support, and the sprints.

# ABOUT THE AUTHOR

Lola King is a dark, steamy romance author who loves giving happy ever after's to antiheroes. She writes about flawed and deeply broken characters, and the women who brings them down to their knees. Her books are sometimes cute, sometimes angsty, but always sexy! Lola lives in London and if she isn't writing, she is most likely keeping her mind busy putting together a play or making music.

Let's keep in touch on IG @lolaking_author or on FB readers' group *Lola's Kings* !